Copyright ©2000 by Nord-Süd Verlag AG, Gossau Zürich, Switzerland
First published in Switzerland under the title *Wer fährt mit ans Meer?*
English translation copyright ©2000 by North-South Books Inc.
Reprinted by permission of North-South Books Inc.
First published in the United States, Great Britain, Canada,
Australia, and New Zealand in 2000 by North-South Books,
an imprint of Nort-Süd Verlag AG, Gossau Zürich, Switzerland.
Distributed in the United States by North-South Books Inc., New York.
Library of Congress Cataloging-in-Publication Data is available.
A CIP catalogue record for this book is available from The British Library.
ISBN 0-7358-1268-3 (trade binding) 10 9 8 7 6 5 4 3 2 1
ISBN 0-7358-1269-1 (library binding) 10 9 8 7 6 5 4 3 2 1

For more information about our books, and the authors
and artists who create them, visit our web site:
www.northsouth.com

Printed in the United States of America

A MICHAEL NEUGEBAUER BOOK

# NORTH-SOUTH BOOKS / NEW YORK / LONDON

# How Will We Get to the Beach?

BRIGITTE LUCIANI
ILLUSTRATED BY
EVE THARLET
TRANSLATED BY
ROSEMARY LANNING

One beautiful summer
day Roxanne decided to
go to the beach.
Everything she wanted to
take with her could be
counted on the fingers
of one hand.

the turtle,
the umbrella,
the thick book
of stories,
the ball, and,
of course, her baby.

But the car wouldn't start.

"Then we'll take the bus to the beach," said Roxanne.

But something couldn't go
with them. What was it?

The little green turtle!

Animals weren't allowed on the bus.
"We can't go to the beach without the turtle!"
cried Roxanne.

"Then we'll ride our bike to the beach," she said.

But something couldn't go with them. What was it?

The orange-spotted ball!

The ball wouldn't fit on the bicycle.
"We can't go to the beach without the ball!"
cried Roxanne.

"hen we'll ride our skateboard to the beach," she said.

3ut something couldn't go with them. What was it?

The big yellow umbrella.

Roxanne didn't have a free hand to hold it.
"We can't go to the beach without the umbrella!"
cried Roxanne.

"Then we'll ride our kayak to the beach," she said.

But something couldn't go with them. What was it?

The thick blue book of stories.

The kayak was very wobbly, and the book might get wet.
"We can't go to the beach without the book!"
cried Roxanne.

"Then we'll fly in a balloon to the beach," she said.

But something couldn't go with them. What was it?

Roxanne's baby!

He wouldn't climb aboard because he was afraid of flying.
"We can't go to the beach without my baby!" cried Roxanne. "He is more important than all the other things. I wouldn't go anywhere without my baby!"

Roxanne sighed. "How will we *ever* get to the beach?"

Just then a farmer passed by with his horse and cart.
He was on his way to the beach to sell cherries.

So they piled aboard:
Roxanne,
the green turtle,
the big yellow umbrella,
the thick blue book of stories,
the orange-spotted ball,
and, of course, her baby.

And they had a wonderful time!